Some Birthday!

Some Birthday!

PATRICIA POLACCO

SIMON & SCHUSTER BOOKS FOR YOUNG READERS

Published by Simon & Schuster

New York·London·Toronto·Sydney·Tokyo·Singapore

SIMON & SCHUSTER BOOKS FOR YOUNG READERS
Simon & Schuster Building, Rockefeller Center, 1230 Avenue of the Americas,
New York, New York 10020.

Designed by Lucille Chomowicz. The text of this book is set in 15 point Usherwood Medium.
The illustrations were done in pencil with color marking pens and acrylic paint.
Manufactured in Hong Kong. 10 9 8 7 6 5 4 3 2

Library of Congress Cataloging-in-Publication Data
Polacco, Patricia. Some birthday! / by Patricia Palacco. Summary: On her birthday Dad takes
a young girl and her brother to see the Monster at Clay Pit Bottoms. [1. Birthdays—
Fiction. 2. Fathers—Fiction.] I. Title. PZ7.P75188Ch 1991 [E]—dc20 90-10381 AC
ISBN 0-671-72750-8

For Pam Pollack

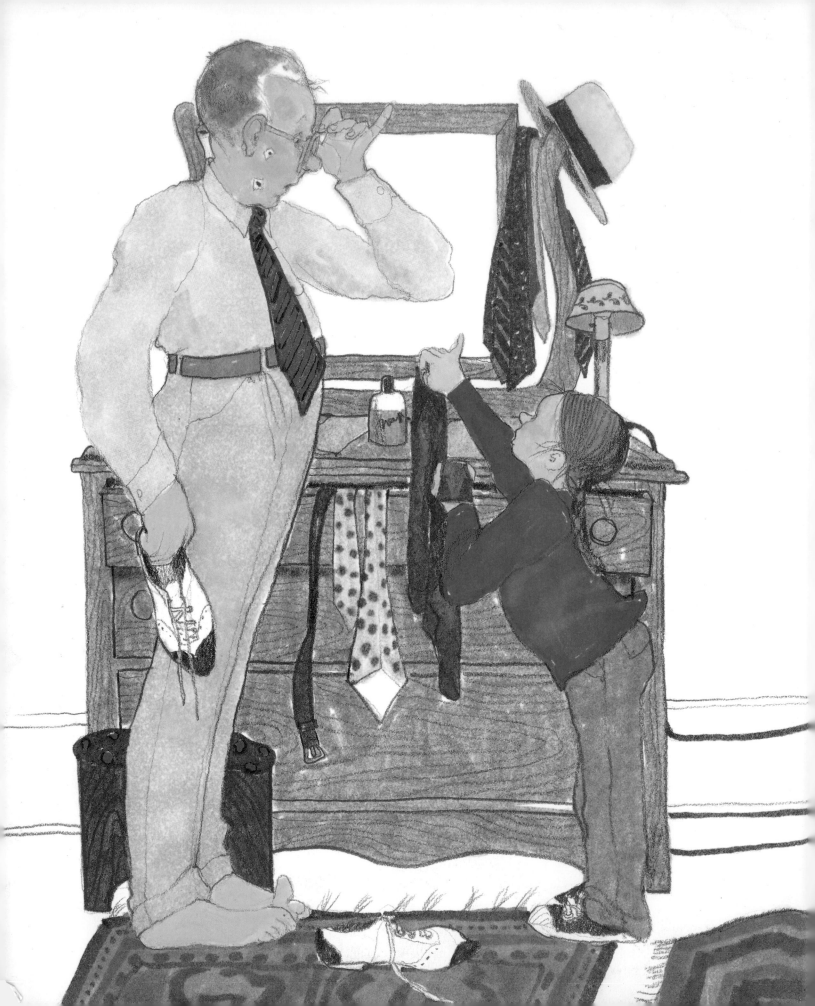

My mom and dad were divorced.

My brother, Rich, and I lived with my mother, except that we spent every summer with Dad and Gramma, my dad's mother. Cousin Billy lived nearby.

Dad was a traveling salesman.

It was my job to get him up and to make sure his socks matched. He was color-blind, you see.

Before he went to work, Dad and I would have breakfast together. We'd talk about everything in the world, and he could always make me laugh. But today he wasn't saying anything—and it was my birthday!

"Anything special happening today, Daddy?" I asked, hoping it would help him remember.

"Nope, honey. Today's about the same as any other day, I'd say."

Just as I was going to drop a big hint about the pedal pushers and blouse I wanted for my birthday, he was out the door, into his car, and off to work.

"See you tonight, honey," he called out.

That night when Dad came home, I looked for a birthday present.

He read the paper like he always did. Then he started watching TV, like he always did!

Suddenly, my dad sat up in his easy chair and got that look in his eye that usually meant he was up to something. "I think tonight might be the perfect night to do it," he said.

"Do what?" my brother and my cousin Billy asked.

"I think tonight we should head down to the Clay Pit."

"But, Dad," I said, "everybody knows that the Clay Pit is haunted!"

"I'm with you, Dad," my brother said.

"Me, too," added Billy.

Not only had my birthday been completely forgotten, but now we had to go to one of the scariest places on earth…and at night!

"Tonight we're going to get the very first photograph ever taken of the Monster at Clay Pit Bottoms."

Even though I was scared, I began to feel a little excited.

"Okay, Richie Boy, you get the bait," Dad told my brother as he read from a list he'd made. "Some smelly cheese will do."

"I'll get some from the fridge," said Gramma.

"You get my camera, Billy," said Dad.

"Okay, Uncle Bill," my cousin called.

"Patricia, you go get the flashlights."

"Got 'em," I called out as I held up two Everlast Midnight Specials.

"Hot dogs. Buns. Marshmallows," my dad read.

"I'll put them in a basket for you and the children, William," said Gramma.

"If we each carry a blanket, we'll be all set," said Dad.

We put on galoshes, rain gear, and woolen caps in case it got cold.

We marched down the street toward the bottomland
at the edge of town.
   "We're almost there," my dad called out in a kind of
scary voice.

As we came up to the edge of the water, it looked black, cold, and very deep.

"I think I saw something," Billy whispered.

We all gasped and stood stock-still as we watched the water for a sign of the monster's approach.

"C'mon, kids," my dad ordered. "We have to set up camp."

We threw our blankets over a low-hanging branch and put rocks on the corners to make a tent. Then we all collected wood for our campfire.

The fire looked warm and friendly.

"Let's eat," Dad said as he threaded hot dogs onto sticks. "We'll need our strength later."

"What do you think the monster looks like?" I asked my father.

He dabbed the mustard from the corners of his mouth.

"Well," he began, "I've heard it's the ugliest, meanest, slimiest thing anyone ever saw. People say that if you look it in the eye, your hair turns white and you're never the same again."

We all just looked at each other, too scared to speak.

"I know that it loves things that smell bad. That's why you kids should never squawk about taking baths."

We all looked at the water for a long time.

"Do you think that if we get its picture, it will get in the papers, Uncle Bill?" my cousin asked after a while.

"Sure! It'll make the *State Journal*...and we'll all be heroes," my dad promised. "Now I think that this is just about the right time for us to begin."

"Begin what?" I said, still scared.

Dad didn't answer.

"It ought to come for this alright," Dad said as he put the smelly cheese on the edge of the pit. "My, but you are brave kids," he said. "Sure can't think of anyone that I'd rather risk my hide with than you!"

Just then something rippled the surface
of the black water.

"See that?" my brother whispered.

"Something really big is out there," I squealed.

My dad's face became very serious. Maybe he was even
a little scared himself.

"What if it comes after us?" my cousin Bill cried.

"If it looks like it's going to come after us, then run with
all your might for home. Don't look back…just keep
running!" my father told us.

Then there was a rustling in the bulrushes. The frogs
stopped croaking.

"I see it!" my brother yelled.

I wasn't sure, but I thought I could see something big gliding along the water straight at us!

Dad took the camera and walked into the darkness to investigate.

Soon we heard snarling and growling. We started screaming and hollering at each other. Then we heard a loud *kerplash*.

I flashed the light at the sound and saw something BIG coming out of the water. It stood on two hind legs and came right at us. It smelled awful!

Then there was a terrible howl.

"It's the monster. Let's get outa here!" my brother shouted as he ran for home.

"The monster!" we all screamed as we ran up on our front porch.

Breathlessly, we told my gramma what had happened.
"Well," she said. "I think your monster is coming through
the front door right now!"
There was my dad, soaked to the skin, smelling real
bad, covered with bulrushes. "You should have seen it,

Ma," my dad told Gramma between belly laughs. "Our monster turned out to be a floating log. Then Harley Beeches's bloodhounds found the cheese and got into a fight. I tried to separate them, slipped, and fell into the water...." Then my old man laughed so hard he cried.

"Some way to celebrate a certain little girl's birthday!" said Gramma as she brought my birthday cake—a whipped cream cake with a rubber monster and candles on top.

Then everybody yelled happy birthday!

"You remembered," I said as I opened my dad's present. "Just what I wanted." The pedal pushers and blouse didn't match, but who could complain...this had been some birthday!

"Daddy, is there really a monster?" I asked.

"Of course there is!" my dad said between mouthfuls of whipped cream cake. "Maybe next year," he said with a wink, "we'll get the picture."

Then everyone sang "Happy Birthday" to me.
My dad sang the loudest—and off-key, of course.
That's my dad.